Oh No, It's Robert

Oh No, It's Robert

Barbara Seuling
Illustrated by Paul Brewer

SCHOLASTIC INC.

New York Toronto London Auckland Sydney
Mexico City New Delhi Hong Kong Buenos Aires

ISBN 0-439-23544-8

12 11 10 9 8 7 6 5   3 4 5 6/0

Printed in the U.S.A.   40

First Scholastic printing, February 2001

Designed by Anthony Jacobson

for Miriam, for everything
—B. S.

for Kathy
—P. B.

Contents

Oh No, It's Robert

The
Pig Stamp

Robert Dorfman hated math. He hated it more than going to the dentist, or eating liver, or cleaning his room.

Here it was, a great day for riding his bike, and Robert was stuck with math homework. He came down the stairs, making a soft *thump, thump* with his sneakers.

Robert's mother had left that afternoon for a travel agents' convention in Florida. He had never stayed alone with just his dad and Charlie before. It was a little weird, like now, when he had to ask his dad to help him with a math problem.

It was easy asking his mom for help, because she didn't mind if he didn't get it right away.

She always made him feel good about something. "I like your drawing of the cucumber," she told him last week. It was supposed to be a spaceship, but it didn't matter, as long as she liked it. She stuck it to the refrigerator with the pineapple magnet.

But Robert's father was a math teacher. He loved math, and naturally he expected Robert to love math, too.

"Hi, Tiger. What's up?" Mr. Dorfman looked up over the newspaper.

"I need some help with my math."

"Sure," said his father. "Here. Sit down." He had a look in his eyes that Robert knew well. It was the look that said, *This time, maybe he'll get it.*

Robert plopped down next to his father on the sofa.

"So. What's the problem?"

Robert glanced at the shelf of sports trophies that his brother, Charlie, had won. On the wall was a Certificate of Excellence from the River Edge Chamber of Commerce with his mother's name on it. There was a plaque naming his father "Teacher of the Year" in Bergen County.

Robert had never won anything. The only things with his name on them were the pencils from Aunt Julie that said HAPPY BIRTHDAY ROBERT.

"Well? Show me," said his father.

Robert pointed to a page in his math book. "It's problem number five," he said.

His father read it out loud. "'There are 6 monkeys in the zoo. The zookeeper has 8 bananas left in one bin. He has 4 bananas in another bin. How many bananas does the zookeeper have, and how many bananas does each monkey get?'

"That's easy. Let's see what you have." Robert's father looked at his notebook, where Robert had written:

$$\begin{array}{r} 8 \\ +\ 4 \\ \hline 12 \end{array}$$

"You're right," his father said. "First you have to add the bananas together. But what do you do next? How do you know how many bananas each monkey gets?"

"Divide?"

"Right," said Mr. Dorfman. "So what do you get?"

"Um . . . a lot of bananas," Robert said. He grinned, hoping his father would think that was funny.

He didn't. "Robert, this is not the time for jokes. Think. What is the answer?"

Robert erased the numbers in his notebook. If he could just get it right, his father could go back to reading his newspaper and he could go for a bike ride. Paul was waiting for him right now so they could go over to Van Saun Park. But his brain just wouldn't work when it came to math.

Robert felt itchy. He knew his father was staring at him, waiting. He tried to remember Mrs. Bernthal's voice as they practiced dividing by six that morning. "Take your time, boys and girls."

Robert scribbled furiously, then erased and scribbled again. He wrote:

$$12\overline{)6}$$

"No, no! You're not thinking, Robert!" Robert saw the little vein in his father's neck jump.

"Oh. Wait a minute." Robert erased his numbers. He scribbled in his notebook again:

$$6\overline{)12}\ \ ^{2}$$

"Two?" he said.

"Are you sure?" asked his father.

Robert looked at his notebook and nodded. His father smiled. "All right," he said. Robert closed his notebook.

"Wait," said his father. "What if the zookeeper had only five monkeys?"

"Huh?"

"What if the zookeeper had twelve bananas to divide among five monkeys?"

"It says six monkeys."

"Yes, I know. But what if it said five?"

Robert felt hot and sweaty. He opened his notebook and sighed. If they were *his* monkeys, he would just let them fight over the bananas. But he knew that was not the answer his father wanted.

"Do it the same way, Robert. Divide the number of bananas by the number of monkeys."

Robert couldn't hear Mrs. Bernthal's voice in his head anymore. He counted on his fingers and wrote down numbers in his notebook. He erased and wrote more numbers.

"Think, Robert. Think."

"Two . . . but there are some left over."

"Aha! Now you've got it!" said his father.

Robert didn't think he had anything. It didn't come out even. He had bananas left, and the poor monkeys were probably still hungry.

He erased the numbers he had scribbled all over the page. He rubbed so hard that he made a hole.

"Don't!" cried his father, but it was too late. "You made a hole in it," he said. He stared at Robert as though he were an alien.

Robert looked at the page. "I know," he said in a tiny voice.

"Robert, always hand in neat work," his father said. "Even if you have to do it over ten times. It tells what kind of person you are. It shows you care."

Robert couldn't believe the fuss his father made over a little hole in the paper. But if it mattered that much to him, he would fix it. "O.K., Dad," he said. He went upstairs two steps at a time and called Paul on his parents' bedroom phone.

"I can't ride my bike today," he said. "I have too much homework."

"It's O.K.," Paul replied. "I have stuff to do, too. We'll go another time."

After Robert hung up, he copied the page with the hole over. He tried very hard not to tear the paper. When he made a mistake, he erased it carefully. If he did make a hole, he started over again. He wanted to show his father—and Mrs. Bernthal—that he was the kind of person who cared.

Robert's homework almost always had COULD BE NEATER! stamped on it with a picture of a pig in a mud puddle. He hated that pig stamp.

It was nearly dark when Robert finally finished his homework. He made only three mistakes on the final sheet of paper. There were little gray clouds around the places where he erased, but there were no holes.

Paper Keys

"I have a special announcement, class," said Mrs. Bernthal. "Please take your seats."

Robert was happy to leave the reading corner. Slow readers had good readers for buddies. Robert was a slow reader and Susanne Lee Rodgers was his reading buddy. She made Robert read every sentence three times, and then she would say, "That's good, Robert!" and smile.

When Susanne Lee smiled at Robert like that, it made him feel like a dodo bird. His father had told him that dodo birds lived a long time ago and were pretty stupid. When people tried to catch dodos to cook and eat, they didn't even try to run away. So now there were no more dodo birds.

Robert walked over to table four and took his seat across from his friend Paul Felcher. Paul's family had moved to River Edge just before school started. Mrs. Bernthal had put Paul and Robert at the same table, and they became friends right away.

Paul's curly head was bent over his notebook. When he wasn't lost in a book, Paul was always drawing spaceships. They never looked like cucumbers as Robert's did. This one was silver and blue and had orange fire coming out of its tail.

Mrs. Bernthal walked around the room, handing out homework papers. She put Robert's homework on the table in front of him. There was no pig stamp on it!

"I have good news, boys and girls," said Mrs. Bernthal. "We are going to have a contest."

"What kind of contest?" asked Susanne Lee.

Mrs. Bernthal went back to her desk and picked up a shiny gold box that looked like a pirate's treasure chest.

"Oh, it's beautiful," said Vanessa Nicolini. "Is it real gold?"

"No, Vanessa, this is not real gold. Nor is this a real key," said Mrs. Bernthal, holding up a key cut out of orange construction paper.

"You mean it's a fake?" shouted Lester Willis from the back of the room.

"No, Lester. This key and the chest are symbols," said Mrs. Bernthal. "They represent the treasures of knowledge that will be open to you if you work and study hard."

Robert listened while he tried to draw a spaceship in his notebook. It looked like a hot dog without the roll. Then he drew a Pilgrim hat. When he finished, it looked more like a witch's hat.

Mrs. Bernthal continued, "I will pin one of these paper keys to the bulletin board with your name on it for each item on this list that you accomplish." She pointed to a sheet of paper fastened to the bulletin board with four silver tacks.

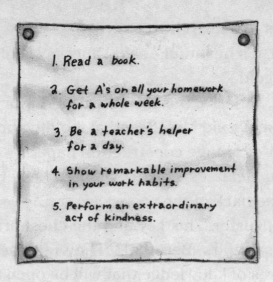

1. Read a book.

2. Get A's on all your homework for a whole week.

3. Be a teacher's helper for a day.

4. Show remarkable improvement in your work habits.

5. Perform an extraordinary act of kindness.

"The boy or girl who has collected the most paper keys three weeks from today—December 4—will win this little chest."

Mrs. Bernthal lifted the page of the calendar to December and circled the 4 with her Big Jumbo red marker. The picture showed children playing in the snow. "I hope you will all try for the treasure chest." She turned the page of the calendar back to November with its picture of the first Thanksgiving.

Robert figured that Susanne Lee would probably win the treasure chest, since she was the smartest person in the class. She even cried once after a spelling test when she found out she spelled one word wrong.

"The winner," said Mrs. Bernthal, "will have his or her name engraved on the chest."

Robert looked up. The shiny gold box lay open on Mrs. Bernthal's desk. Inside, a tiny gold key lay on a lining of red velvet. He could picture it in the living room next to all the other awards his family had won. He could imagine his father pointing to it with pride and saying, "My son Robert won that. He's a person who cares."

Robert read the list again. "Read a book." No way. That could take forever.

He looked at number 2. "Get A's on all your homework for a whole week." Robert was in the slow reading group, he hated math, and he was a bad speller. Better not think about that one.

Number 3 seemed O.K. "Be a teacher's helper for a day." Robert was a pretty good helper at home. He took out the garbage every Thursday and set the table sometimes. And now, while his mother was away, he made his own breakfast and helped with the dishes.

He read number 4. "Show remarkable improvement in your work habits." He thought of how hard it was just to do his homework without making holes in the paper.

Number 5 sounded interesting. "Perform an extraordinary act of kindness." What would he have to do? He wasn't sure.

He went back to number 3. All day long, Robert thought of ways to help Mrs. Bernthal. He helped her give out paper for spelling. He sharpened her pencils. He even emptied the pencil sharpener.

At the end of the day, Mrs. Bernthal said, "I have one more announcement, class. Tomorrow you will see a big basket in the hall by the front door. The PTA will put a turkey in that basket just before Thanksgiving. In the meantime, we are asking you to bring in nonperishable food to fill up the basket. It will provide a dinner for a family who might otherwise go hungry on Thanksgiving Day."

"Will we get a paper key for bringing in something for the basket?" asked Susanne Lee.

"No," said Mrs. Bernthal. "This is our way of sharing with someone less fortunate than ourselves. It's an act of kindness and comes from the heart. It is not for personal gain."

Robert was glad Susanne Lee asked that question. He had been wondering the same thing.

"O.K., it's almost three o'clock. It's a good time to choose a book to take home."

Chairs scraped the floor and papers flew off the tables as a few children got up to go to the library corner. Robert picked up the papers.

"Why thank you, Robert," said Mrs. Bernthal.

"Um, sure," he said.

Robert went over to the classroom library, a corner in the back of the room made by two tall bookcases. A couple of cushions on the floor made it cozy. Paul was looking through a colorful illustrated book about Neptune.

Robert picked the skinniest book he could find. The title was *Moths*. He showed it to Mrs. Bernthal. "That looks interesting," she said, writing the title on her library list. As Robert slipped the book into his book bag, Susanne Lee bounced over to Mrs. Bernthal's desk.

"I'm taking out two books, Mrs. Bernthal," she said.

"All right, Susanne Lee, let me sign them out." She wrote down the titles of Susanne Lee's books. One was about the first Thanksgiving and the other was a story about a baby-sitting club.

Paul signed out the book on Neptune. Robert could see that he would never win the treasure chest this way. Even if he finished the book on moths, he could never read as many books as Susanne Lee or Paul. He must be crazy for thinking he could win that prize.

"When is Mom coming home?" asked Robert's brother, Charlie, that evening at the dinner table. He stared at the round black thing that looked like a hockey puck on his plate.

"She'll be home Monday morning," said his father. "Sorry the hamburgers got overdone."

Robert tried to cut into his hamburger with the side of his fork, but it wouldn't cut. He picked it up and nibbled at the edges. After he chewed through the black part and dipped it in catsup, it wasn't too bad.

Charlie left his hamburger on his plate and only ate his French fries.

"You have to eat more than that," said his father.

"It's O.K., Dad," said Charlie. "I had a really big lunch today and a humongous snack after school. May I be excused? I have a lot of homework."

"Well, O.K.," said Mr. Dorfman. "It's Robert's turn to help me with the dishes tonight."

Robert helped clear the table and rinse the plates the way his father showed him. Together, they loaded the dishwasher. Everything had to be put in just so.

"So, how is the math going?" asked Robert's father.

"O.K., I guess," said Robert. "Dad?"

"What, Tiger?"

"How come Mom has to be gone so long?"

"It's this new job," said his father. "She wants to be a really good travel agent. This convention is where she can learn about the travel business. It's only for four days."

"And after that she can stay home with us?"

"Yes," said Robert's father with a sigh. He poured soap powder into the little cup on the dishwasher door. "I sure hope so. I miss her, too."

The dishwasher began to rumble. Mr. Dorfman went into the living room and settled down in front of the TV to watch the news.

Robert went up to his room. He unzipped his book bag and the book on moths fell out. When he opened it, he saw that every single page had been scribbled on with a bright green marker.

The Five Food Groups

"**W**hat's that?" Susanne Lee Rodgers cried.

Robert looked at the package he had just put in the Thanksgiving food basket. "Chocolate-covered jelly cookies," he said.

"Oh, Robert!" said Susanne Lee with that dodo-bird smile. "Don't you know you're supposed to bring *real* food for the basket?" She placed a bottle of cranberry juice on top of the other food. Vanessa dropped a can of corn niblets next to it.

"Cookies are real," said Paul.

"You can't give cookies to a poor family!" Susanne Lee said.

"Why? Don't poor people like cookies?"

asked Robert.

"Of course they *like* cookies," said Susanne Lee. "But you have to give them nutritious food, like vegetables. Or fruit. Something from one of the five food groups."

"Mrs. Bernthal just said to bring food."

"Nonperishable food," added Paul.

Robert couldn't even remember the five food groups. They had learned about them in a movie in Assembly. He was pretty sure cookies weren't in any of them.

"Maybe they never get to have cookies, if they're so poor," said Paul. "Then it would be nice if someone gave them some for Thanksgiving."

Susanne Lee sighed. "You boys are pitiful," she said. Her hair bounced as she walked away.

"I don't get it," said Robert. "I'd rather have cookies than cranberry juice, wouldn't you?"

"Yeah," said Paul. "Are you taking the cookies back?"

"No, but I'll bring in something else. Maybe Susanne Lee is wrong." But he knew better— Susanne Lee was never wrong.

"Let's see how you are doing with your keys," said Mrs. Bernthal later that day. She went to the bulletin board, where the paper keys were pinned. There was a lot of rustling as everyone settled down in the classroom.

"Susanne Lee gets a key for marking the homework for me, and another for reading a book. Did you read the book from cover to cover?"

"Yes," said Susanne Lee. "But someone scribbled all over it."

"Oh, that's a shame," said Mrs. Bernthal. "Who would do such a terrible thing? Books are our friends. Why would anyone want to hurt a friend?" Robert remembered the scribbles in his book on moths. Would Mrs. Bernthal think he did it?

Mrs. Bernthal continued, "And Paul gets one, too, for reading a book." Robert looked at Paul in awe. The contest had just been announced yesterday.

"Excellent," said Mrs. Bernthal, pinning up a paper key. "And you get two keys, Robert. You helped me with chores in the classroom yesterday and today."

"Mother's little helper," called a voice from the back of the room. That could only be Lester Willis. He always called people names.

"Ignore him," whispered Paul.

"Yeah," Robert agreed. Lester was a bully and a tease. There was no point in messing with him.

Robert looked at the paper keys with his name on them. It felt good to see that he had as many as Susanne Lee.

"A reminder, class," said Mrs. Bernthal. "Inventions Day is a week from Monday. Your reports will be due. Remember, you have to talk about an invention that made life easier for many people."

At the end of the day, Robert and Paul stood on the steps in front of the school. It was cloudy and gray and had been raining off and on all day.

"It's not a bike day," said Paul.

"Too bad," said Robert. "I don't have to do homework today. I have all weekend to do it."

"Me, too," said Paul.

"Can you come to my house?" asked Robert. He didn't want to go home alone. The house would be too empty until Charlie and his dad came home.

"O.K.," said Paul. "But I have to call my mother."

They pulled up the hoods on their rain ponchos and walked the four blocks to Robert's house.

The house looked dark and quiet. Robert opened the door with his key and locked it behind them. He and Paul threw their book bags on the stairs.

"There's always somebody in my house," said Paul, "except when my brother, Nick, was born. Then my mom was at the hospital for three days. I was glad when she came home. While she was gone my dad made sardines for dinner."

"Really?" Robert shuddered at the thought of eating sardines for dinner. He hated sardines. "My mother will be home soon," he told Paul. It helped to say it.

After Paul called his mother, they looked for a snack. Robert opened the kitchen cabinet. He had taken the package of chocolate-covered jelly cookies for the food basket at school. "There's nothing in here except some stale potato chips," he said. Obviously, his dad hadn't done the grocery shopping yet.

"What about the refrigerator?" asked Paul.

"Let's look," said Robert. The container of milk was almost empty. There was half a bottle of seltzer, some Diet Delight bread, a jar of strawberry jam, and some white cheese on a plate.

"Good. Cream cheese," said Robert.

They put two slices of the Diet Delight bread on a plate. Paul bit a corner off his slice.

"This tastes like straw," he said.

"Maybe it will taste better with the cream cheese," said Robert.

They spread the cheese on the bread and covered it with strawberry jam. They bit into their slices at the same time. "YUCK!" cried Paul. "It's spoiled!"

They ran to the sink and took turns holding their mouths open under the faucet. Robert could not wash the taste of the cheese out of his mouth. "Maybe if we drink something . . . ," he said.

They poured some seltzer into glasses and gulped it down. "Ugh!" said Paul. "What kind of seltzer is this?"

Robert read the label. "It says G-R-A-P-E-F-R—"

"Grapefruit!" Paul ran for the sink again.

Robert saw a folded-up label sticking out from under the cheese. He pulled it out. This time he had no trouble reading it.

"It's GOAT CHEESE!"

"Oh no!" cried Paul.

They ran into the bathroom and spit noisily into the sink. Robert found strong red mouthwash and they rinsed their mouths out with it. Then, just to be safe, they rubbed peppermint-flavored toothpaste on their teeth and rinsed some more.

When the taste of the goat cheese was finally gone, they went up to Robert's room, taking the potato chips with them. There they flopped down together on Robert's beanbag chair and nibbled on the stale chips.

"Did you pick your invention yet?" asked Robert.

"Spaceships," said Paul.

"How did spaceships make life easier for people?"

"We got satellite TV and weather stations."

"Yeah, I guess so," said Robert. "I don't know what to pick."

"How about computers?"

"No."

"The telephone?"

"Uh-uh."

"Yeah, those are boring," said Paul. He punched at the beanbag chair. "You probably want to do something more interesting, something that nobody else will think of."

Robert shrugged. "I guess so."

"Don't worry. You'll come up with something. It's probably right under your nose and you don't realize it."

"Yeah. Who do you think will win the treasure chest?" asked Robert.

"Susanne Lee, probably," said Paul.

"Yeah. She'll get a hundred paper keys at least," said Robert. "I was going to try for the treasure chest until I realized that."

Paul didn't even laugh. "Really?" he said.

"I thought I could get lots of paper keys for being a teacher's helper."

"Maybe you could," said Paul. "But you'd have to be a super helper to beat Susanne Lee Rodgers!"

"What do you mean . . ." Robert rolled over in the beanbag chair. "*Super* helper?"

"A helper like no one has ever seen before," said Paul. "A helper who does the job faster and better than anyone else. A helper who thinks of little extra things that teachers would like . . ."

Robert rolled back again and frowned. "Hmmm. And you really think I could do it?"

"Yeah, but I think you'd have to advertise," said Paul.

"Huh?"

"Advertise! Hand out fliers to all the teachers."

"What kind of fliers?" Robert asked, thinking of airplanes.

"The kind my dad gets printed up for his cleaning business. I have one here in my notebook. I used the other side for a drawing."

Paul flipped through his notebook and pulled it out. The flier said:

"See?" said Paul. "They're like little posters, telling how good you are. You can hand them out to all the teachers. Wait a second, I'll show you." Paul opened his notebook and wrote something across a page. "Here," he said, handing the paper to Robert. It said:

HIRE
ROBERT DORFMAN
SUPER HELPER

Robert stared at his name printed on the page. "It looks good," he said, "but it needs more. You said we have to tell them how good a helper I'd be."

"O.K. Let me think about it. I can make a bunch of these," said Paul. "In color. I'll have them ready on Monday."

"Terrific!" said Robert. "Do you really think I could win?"

"Sure," said Paul. "My father says you can do anything if you really work at it."

Robert sank back into the beanbag chair. Advertise. What a neat idea. Wouldn't his father be pleased! He suddenly sat forward again.

"What if Susanne Lee thinks of fliers, too?"

"She won't," said Paul.

"Why not?"

"She's too busy memorizing the five food groups."

They fell off the beanbag chair, laughing.

Super Helper

On Monday morning, Robert stared at one of the fliers Paul handed to him. Except for a smudge in the upper right corner, it was gorgeous.

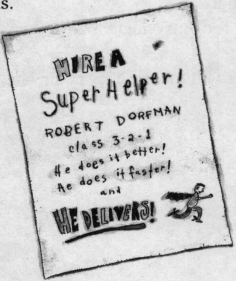

The letters were in all different colors. Next to the letters was a little man in a red cape running across the page. He had little wings on his feet.

"Did you draw this yourself?" asked Robert. Paul nodded.

"It's really good."

"Thanks. Sorry about the smudge. Nick tried to grab the paper while I was drawing."

"That's O.K.," said Robert. "What does 'HE DELIVERS' mean?"

"I don't know. I copied it from my father's flier."

At lunchtime, Robert and Paul handed out fliers to all the teachers on the second and third floors. By the end of the day, Robert and Paul both had jobs with Mrs. Gold, the music teacher. She said she could use help moving band instruments and music stands to the auditorium on Assembly mornings. That meant getting up early and being at school before the other kids on Wednesdays.

Mrs. Ruskin asked Robert to take papers to the office every day at lunchtime. Mr. Lobel asked Robert to clean out the animal cages in the science room once a week.

The best job came after lunch. Mrs. Bernthal had Robert's flier on her desk. "Robert," she said, "I was thinking that we need a library monitor, and I'm sure you're just the man for the job. What do you think? Would you like to take care of our classroom books?"

"Sure," said Robert, turning to catch Paul's eye.

"Maybe that will keep our books safe," she said. "We need someone who will care about them and see that they are handled properly. Everything is a hodgepodge now. Maybe you can put the books in alphabetical order."

Someone who cares. Robert remembered his father's words and smiled. As he took his seat, Paul reached over and gave him a high-five. "It worked!" he whispered.

"Yeah!" Robert answered.

Suddenly a wad of paper landed on their table. Robert picked it up and opened it. It was one of Paul's fliers. On the back was a drawing skull and crossbones made with a black marker. Robert turned around and saw Lester Willis staring right at him.

All the way home, Robert thought about inventions. As he turned up the walk to his house, he still had no idea what invention he would talk about.

The door was unlocked. "Hello?" he called, expecting Charlie to answer.

"Hello yourself," was the reply.

"Mom?"

"Yes. Mom. Remember me?"

"Mom!" Robert was so happy to see her he dropped his book bag and ran to give her a hug.

"Well, what a welcome! I'll have to go away more often!"

"No!" said Robert, hoping he didn't sound like a baby. His mother squeezed him tight.

"Oh, Robbie, it's good to see you. I missed you. I have so much to tell you—and I want to hear what you've been doing. I still have to make phone calls and write up my report. I'm sure you have homework, so let's save our news and meet back here at . . ." She looked at her watch and winked at him. "Dinnertime," she finished.

"Great!" Robert scooped up his book bag and bounded up the stairs. Having his mom home was what really mattered. He could hold off a little longer with all his news.

As he passed Charlie's room, Robert saw his brother in his red-and-yellow hockey shirt. He looked like a porcupine in his buzz cut. Charlie was tightening the screws on his ice skates.

"Yo, Rob," called Charlie.

"Hi," said Robert, heading for his room.

"Hey. Slow down!" said Charlie.

"I can't. I have work to do," said Robert, but he stopped at the door of Charlie's room anyway.

"What's so important?"

"I have to find an invention to talk about for next week."

"What kind of invention?"

"It has to be something that made life easier for a lot of people."

Charlie tried to wiggle the blade of his skate and then put it down. "I know something you can talk about."

"Really? What is it?"

"The most important invention I can think of is . . . the toilet."

"The toilet?" Robert repeated.

"I'm serious, Rob. Nobody ever talks about it, yet how would we live without it? Think about what it was like before the toilet was invented. People used holes in the ground."

"Holes? No kidding?" asked Robert.

"No kidding," said Charlie. "Then they made little wooden houses above the holes. If you had to go to the bathroom in the middle of the night, you had to go out in your pajamas. You had to sit in the cold and dark. Maybe there was rain or snow or lightning. Or even wild animals." Charlie wrinkled his nose. "It smelled pretty bad, too."

"I don't know," Robert said. The toilet seemed like a pretty weird invention to talk about. But Paul did say it should be unusual. And he also said it would probably be right under his nose.

"Ask anyone, Rob," continued Charlie. "We're pretty lucky to have the toilet. It's a great invention. Other people might think the radio, or the printing press, or the car are more important. But I'd rather have a toilet than any of those things." He picked up his other skate.

Robert thought about that. He'd rather have a toilet than a printing press. Or even a car, because he couldn't drive yet. He thought about the radio. He liked his Sony Walkman, but maybe he'd rather have a toilet on a cold winter night.

"O.K. Thanks." Robert went to his room. He opened the "T" volume of the encyclopedia. He found TOGA and TOOLS and TOYS, but TOILET wasn't there. So he tried to remember what Charlie said and wrote it down.

At dinner his mother handed everyone a T-shirt with palm trees and "Fort Lauderdale" printed on the front.

"So, what great truths did you discover about the travel business?" asked Robert's dad, spooning some filling into his taco shell.

"That everyone needs a vacation—even travel agents," said Mrs. Dorfman with a laugh.

"But you were in Florida," said Charlie. "Wasn't that like a vacation?"

"Not really. We were going to meetings from eight in the morning till eight or nine at night . . .

all inside our air-conditioned hotel. There was a pool, but by the time I got back to my room at night, all I could think of was stretching out across the bed, and the next thing I knew, I was getting a wake-up call to start the next day of meetings."

"You mean you didn't see Disney World?" asked Robert.

"No," said his mother. "We were nowhere near Disney World. Besides, I wouldn't have had any fun there without you."

After dinner Robert went back to his room and looked at his notes for his report. He felt funny talking about toilets, but Charlie was right. It sure was a better world with them.

There was a knock, and his mother opened the door. "Hi, Robbie," she said. "Mind if I come in?"

"Sure," he said. "I mean . . . no." He picked up his notes. Maybe he could talk to his mother about his report.

She stopped to look closely at a copy of Robert's flier taped to the wall. "This is good, Robert."

"Paul made it," said Robert, pleased.

"Did it work?"

"Yes. I'm the library monitor and cleanup helper for Mrs. Bernthal, and I help Mrs. Gold with musical instruments on Assembly Day, and I help Mrs. Ruskin with errands and Mr. Lobel in the science room."

"That's pretty ambitious! I'm sure you do an excellent job, too." She looked around. "Did you finish your homework?"

Robert nodded. He didn't want to tell his mother about the treasure chest—yet.

"Have you practiced your reading?"

"A little," he said. He picked up his book on moths and showed it to her. Actually, he had only looked at the pictures so far.

"Good," she said, looking at the gypsy moth on the cover. "I know things have been difficult for you lately, Robbie. I've been so busy with the convention, and now we have a new advertising campaign. But it will be over soon. I have to finish up this one last report. Then I'll be home at a normal hour every night. And I'll have more time to spend with you."

"That's great, Mom," he said.

"Is everything O.K.?" she asked. "Is there anything we need to talk about?"

Robert didn't want to bother her if she was busy with her report. "It can wait, Mom," he said.

She got up and planted a kiss on his forehead. "You're terrific!" she said. "I'll see you later, to kiss you good-night."

It was great having his mom home, but she was busy almost all the time. Robert practiced his talk on Stanley, his model stegosaur. Whenever he said the word "toilet" out loud he got stuck. It was embarrassing to say that word in front of your whole class. Was there another word he could use?

He looked up "toilet" in the dictionary, but that was no help. It said toilet was "1. a dressing table. 2. the process of grooming oneself." and "3. equipped with a water closet." Water closet? He looked that up. "A small room with a flush toilet in it. Abbreviated w.c." That was more like it, although he had never heard a toilet referred to as a water closet before.

Robert worked on his talk every day. He thought about practicing in front of his dad, but he remembered the math problem and changed his mind. He recited it once more to

44

Stanley before he went to bed Sunday night. He thought it was missing something, but he couldn't figure out what it was.

Pink Underwear

Inventions Day was here at last. Robert was ready. Mrs. Bernthal asked for the first volunteer. Susanne Lee Rodgers waved her hand.

"All right, Susanne Lee. You start us off."

Susanne Lee went up to the front of the room, carrying a small lamp. Robert watched her hair bounce as she walked. Mrs. Bernthal helped her plug the lamp into a wall socket near the blackboard.

Susanne Lee wrote THE ELECTRIC LIGHT on the blackboard in big letters. She clicked on the lamp.

"We use electric lights every day," she began. Susanne Lee must have read forty books on Thomas Edison and the electric light bulb for her report. By the time she was finished, Robert felt as though he had read forty books, too. Her report was packed with information. When she finished, Susanne Lee clicked off the lamp.

Matt Blakey followed Susanne Lee. "My invention is the car," he announced, passing around several model cars. He had charts from car manufacturers showing the latest models, and posters of racing cars from the Indy 500. Everyone really liked looking at them.

Paul went next. "This is a spaceship," he said, holding up a drawing. It showed a spaceship cut open so you could see inside.

That was what was missing! Robert thought. He needed something to show, something that got people's attention. It made the talk more interesting. It was his turn next. He had to think fast.

Robert went up to the front of the room and picked up a piece of chalk. He drew a circle on the blackboard. Then he drew another circle inside that one.

"It's a doughnut!" called Matt Blakey. "That's a great invention!"

"Be quiet, class," said Mrs. Bernthal.

Robert added another circle above the first one. He drew in a bottom.

He wrote the water closet in big letters next to it.

"Oh no," whispered Susanne Lee loudly. "He's talking about the *toilet!*" The rest of the class burst out laughing. Mrs. Bernthal clapped her hands to get the class to settle down.

"Everyone needs a toilet," Robert began. Once the word "toilet" was out, he might as well use it. The class broke up.

"Class! Class!" shouted Mrs. Bernthal. "Go on, Robert," she said.

Robert continued. "In the old days, people didn't use toilets," he said. "They used holes in the ground or bushes."

The class exploded again. Robert heard Vanessa hiccuping with laughter. He had to yell to be heard. "LATER, PEOPLE HAD TO GO OUTSIDE AND SIT IN LITTLE HOUSES THEY BUILT AROUND THE HOLES. AT NIGHT, MAYBE THEY TOOK ALONG A FLASHLIGHT."

Mrs. Bernthal rapped on her desk with a ruler. "Where are your manners?" she said to the class.

"In the toilet!" shouted Lester Willis from the back of the room. More laughter, and the lights flashed off and on as Mrs. Bernthal tried to restore order.

Robert felt the heat in his cheeks, but he only had one more line, so he pushed on. "Um, there were many improvements made to the toilet, and that made life easier for a lot of people."

"Thank you, Robert," said Mrs. Bernthal.

"Great show, Toilet Brain!" called Lester. A paper wad flew past him as Robert went back to his seat.

Vanessa was still hiccuping. "Your . . . HIC . . . talk was . . . HIC . . . funny, Robert."

Robert wasn't trying to be funny. He wished he could flush himself—or better still, his brother, Charlie—down the toilet.

At three o'clock, Robert stayed behind to tidy up the library bookshelves before he went home. Paul was waiting for him at the front door when he finally left.

"You didn't have to wait for me," said Robert.

"That's O.K.," replied Paul.

It had rained, and the streets were wet. "You

gave a really interesting talk," Paul said, walking around a puddle.

Robert thought Paul was just being kind. Everyone else had laughed at him. His talk stank. He would never win any paper keys now. He sloshed right through the puddle.

Lester came bouncing up behind them. "Hey, Toilet Face!" he shouted.

"Oh, go away," Robert mumbled.

"What did you say?"

Robert knew right away he was in trouble. No one told Lester Willis to go away.

"Nothing," said Robert.

"You said something," Lester insisted.

"No, I didn't."

"You did." Lester pushed Robert, and Robert stumbled backward.

"Hey, quit that!" called Paul.

Lester moved toward Paul.

Robert dropped his book bag. "Watch this for me," he said to Paul as he stepped between them. The next thing Robert knew, Lester was on top of him, and he was in a mud puddle.

Robert felt the air being squeezed out of him. Lester was like an elephant. Robert tried to push Lester, but that didn't budge him. He pulled at Lester's clothes, and suddenly Lester's pants came unbuttoned. Robert's eyes opened wide. Lester's underwear was pink.

"Hey, Lester," gasped Robert. "Your underwear is showing."

Lester looked down at his open pants and jumped up. Robert was glad to breathe again. Lester clutched his pants and buttoned them. He looked around. "What are you staring at?" Lester roared at Paul.

"Me? Nothing. It's . . . it's . . ."

"It's WHAT?" said Lester.

"It's . . . a nice day," said Paul.

"Yeah," said Robert. "It sure is."

Lester zipped up his jacket. Muttering under his breath, he walked away.

Paul came over. "What happened?" he asked. "Are you O.K.?"

Robert got up out of the mud puddle. "I'm fine," he said. "I guess he decided it was too messy to kill me." It seemed Paul hadn't noticed Lester's pink underwear, and for some reason, Robert couldn't tell him.

Robert looked down. There was mud all over his pants, and he was wet from the puddle.

"You want to come to my house to clean up?" asked Paul.

Robert thought it over. His mother was at the office, Charlie was at hockey practice, and his dad wouldn't be home from school yet. "O.K.," he replied.

"What have you boys been up to?" asked Paul's mother when she saw Robert. Paul's little brother, Nick, was clinging to her leg.

"A fight," answered Paul.

"Really? Fights are for stupid people. Surely you boys are not stupid."

"No, Mom, but the other guy is," said Paul.

"All right. I'll take your word for it," said Mrs. Felcher. "Go wash up, Robert. Take off those pants and let me see what I can do with them. Let's clean you up a bit before you go home. We don't want to scare your mother to death."

Robert went into the bathroom. He didn't know what to do. He knew Mrs. Felcher, but should he take off his pants? Then what? Walk around in someone else's house in his underwear?

He swished the water around in the sink and got his hands good and soapy. There was a knock on the door. Was Paul's mother going to come in and make him take his pants off?

"It's only me," said Paul. He came in with a pair of jeans. "They're mine. I hope they fit you."

"Thanks," said Robert. He finished cleaning up and put the jeans on. They were only a little bit long. He rolled them up.

In the kitchen, Paul's mother was rolling out piecrusts. Nick sat in his booster chair playing with leftover dough. Something bubbled in a pot on the stove.

"Pies," Mrs. Felcher explained. "Four different kinds. For Thanksgiving." The smells were so good Robert's mouth watered.

"There are some cookies on the table," Mrs. Felcher said. "Help yourself to some milk. And don't worry, I'll have your pants ready before you go home."

Paul set out glasses and poured the milk.

"I wish my mother was making pies," said Robert, gulping down his milk. "I don't even know if we're having Thanksgiving this year."

"How come?" asked Paul. "Everyone has

Thanksgiving, even poor families. That's why we're filling the food basket at school."

"Well, I heard her tell someone on the phone she wasn't making a turkey this year."

"Gee," said Paul.

Robert thought of Paul's family eating turkey and four kinds of pie. What would his family eat for Thanksgiving? Tacos? Hot dogs? Robert imagined his dad carving a hot dog into four neat pieces. Then he imagined nibbling stale potato chips and goat cheese. Yuck! Just the thought of that cheese made his tongue curl.

After they finished their cookies, they went to Paul's room. Paul sat on the bed while Robert looked at his drawings of spaceships that hung on the walls. The spaceships were in all colors, purples and blues and reds, with jets of yellow and orange moving them through space. Stars and planets lit up the dark sky behind them. The drawings were the most beautiful that Robert had ever seen.

There was a big box of colored markers on Paul's desk. Some spilled out of the box, reminding Robert of a rainbow.

"I've never seen so many colors in one set of markers," said Robert. No wonder Paul's pictures were so beautiful.

"Yeah," said Paul. "I got them for my birthday. There are more colors than I ever had before."

After a while, Paul's mother came upstairs holding Robert's pants with one hand and Nick with the other.

"Here you are," she said, handing Robert his pants. "Much improved. I ran them through the washer and dryer."

"Thanks," said Robert. As he pulled on his clean pants, he thought about how nice it would be to come home to a house like Paul's, where someone was always around. Did every kid think somebody else's life was better? He decided that no one would wish for his life, with a mom who went on business trips, a dad who loved math, and a brother with the worst ideas in the world.

The Scribbler
Strikes Again

It was still dark when Robert left his house on Assembly Day morning to help Mrs. Gold set up the band instruments. Paul was on his corner waiting for him.

"I was the first one up," said Robert, yawning.

"Not in my house," replied Paul. "My brother smacked me with his teddy bear at six o'clock."

The schoolyard was empty, but the lights in the building were on. They went inside. Robert stopped at the Thanksgiving basket. "Do you think this is real food?" he asked, placing a can of lima beans on top of the pile.

Paul looked. "They must be," he said, making a face. "My mother always wants me to eat them."

A lot of food had been added since the last time Robert walked by. There were cheese curls, oranges, green beans, Spaghetti-Os, candy corn, nuts, butterscotch pudding, candied yams, crackers, and a jar of pickles. He was sure some of those things were not in the five food groups.

There were voices coming from the music room. In the doorway, Robert saw Susanne Lee talking to Mrs. Gold. What was she doing here this early?

"Oh, hello, Robert. Hello, Paul. You're up early this morning," she said sweetly. Robert felt his stomach do a little flip.

"We're here to help Mrs. Gold," he said.

"Oh, good. Then you can carry those big instruments and I'll carry the music stands," Susanne Lee said.

Bossy as usual, Robert thought, lifting a tuba. Paul took the bass drum. Didn't Susanne Lee get enough paper keys reading all those books and getting A's on her homework? She had more paper keys than anyone else. Did she have to be a teacher's helper, too? They went back and forth several times before they had all the equipment in the auditorium.

"You're as fast and as good as you said you were," said Mrs. Gold to Robert. He smiled, feeling pleased with himself.

In their classroom, Robert and Paul took their seats at table four. Paul took out a piece of paper and began drawing, as usual.

"What are you drawing?" Robert whispered.

"This," said Paul, holding up the paper. It was the Mars Special, a purple rocket with turquoise stripes that he had copied from a book on space travel lying next to him on the table. There was a bright yellow sky behind the spaceship.

Paul made such beautiful pictures, Robert thought. Maybe if he could draw like that, he wouldn't need to win a treasure chest. He picked up the space travel book and flipped through it.

The book was all scribbled. Robert saw bright orange zigzags on page after page. It reminded him of Paul's colored markers.

"Robert and Paul, are you listening?" Mrs. Bernthal's voice came through Robert's thoughts. "Copy these new spelling words into your notebooks."

Robert took out his notebook and tried to concentrate on his spelling. Paul was his best friend, and he loved books. He couldn't possibly be the Scribbler . . . could he?

"I like your advertisement," said Miss Valentine as Robert walked into the art room with the rest of his class later that day. She held up his flier. "Do you really deliver what you promise?"

"I . . . I guess so," he said.

"Good. Then you can be my art helper. Come. You can help me give out the supplies."

Another job! Robert looked around for Paul, but he was already at his table spreading out his pencils.

Robert followed Miss Valentine to the tall metal supply cabinet in the back of the room. She opened it and handed him a stack of paper. Robert stared at her long red nails and the rings on her fingers. "Give one of these to each person, please," she said.

Robert went around the room, putting a sheet of paper in front of each boy and girl. Susanne Lee gave hers back.

"This one has fingerprints on it. I want a clean one."

Robert gave her a clean sheet of paper. At least she wasn't trying to be the art helper.

"Today, class," said Miss Valentine, "we are going to make fish prints. Fish played an important part in the first Thanksgiving." She unwrapped a package of four fish and laid them on some newspaper.

"EE-YEW!" cried Vanessa.

"We always hear about turkey and pumpkins and corn," said Miss Valentine, "but we forget about fish. The Pilgrims survived in part because the Native Americans showed them good places to fish."

Miss Valentine wiped the fish with a wet paper towel and patted them dry as she talked. "Robert, will you get out the printing inks and rollers, please? They're on the second shelf of the supply cabinet."

Robert went to the back of the room and opened the cabinet. He saw the box of printing inks and the rollers. He put the rollers in the box and brought everything to the front of the room.

Miss Valentine squeezed a little red ink from one of the tubes onto a plastic tray. She picked up one of the rollers and rolled it through the ink until it was covered with red. Then she used the wet roller to cover the fish in ink.

"YUCK!" said Lester, holding his nose.

"These fish are fresh," said Miss Valentine. "They don't smell bad." She put the roller down and placed a piece of paper on the fish. "The idea," she said, "is to get ink over one whole side of the fish. Then, while the ink is still wet, you press your paper on the fish."

She rolled the clean roller across the paper on top of the fish. She went over and around, spreading the ink evenly. "Press gently, but hard enough to get the ink to stick to the paper." She lifted the paper carefully. "When you lift the paper, the scales of the fish will have made a beautiful pattern." Miss Valentine held up the paper, and there was a gorgeous red fish on it.

"I want to do one! I want to do one!" cried the boys and girls.

"You will all get to make one," promised Miss Valentine. She walked to the back of the room, where a clothesline was stretched from one wall to the other. She carefully hung the red fish print on the clothesline with two clothespins.

"There are four fish and eight rollers and printing inks in lots of different colors. You will have to take turns using the fish and the rollers," she said. "When you are finished, give me your fish and rollers to wash off in the sink for the next person."

Robert chose blue-green ink for his fish. As Miss Valentine walked around the room, she stopped at his table. "Robert, that's an excellent choice," she said. "One thinks of the sea when one looks at your picture."

Paul's fish was red and purple. He was the only one who mixed two colors on his print.

"Beautiful work, Paul," Miss Valentine said.

Once everyone had made a print and hung it on the clothesline to dry, Miss Valentine had them start cleaning up. "Wet a paper towel and wipe off your table, class," she said.

Robert looked at the piles of paper towels and wet newspaper. What a mess! He wanted to show Miss Valentine that he delivered what he promised.

He went around the room collecting the soggy paper towels and threw them in the trash basket. Then he wet a big sponge and cleaned off the big table in the front of the room. He washed the ink off the rollers and plastic trays and fish in the sink. He screwed the caps back on all the tubes of ink and put the inks in the box. He put all the supplies away in the tall steel cabinet and shut the doors. He even swept the floor with the broom that Miss Valentine kept in the corner.

As the class left to go back to Mrs. Bernthal's room, Miss Valentine handed them their dry fish prints.

"Thank you, Robert. That was a job well done." Robert felt Miss Valentine's hand on his shoulder. He could just imagine all those paper keys piling up for being such a good art helper. But he didn't know what to say.

"Um . . . Happy Thanksgiving, Miss Valentine."

"And to you, too, Robert."

Robert ran back to Mrs. Bernthal's room. The class was noisily packing up for the long Thanksgiving weekend.

"Whose turn is it to take Trudy?" asked Mrs. Bernthal. Trudy was the class hamster.

"Mine! Mine!" shouted several voices from across the room.

"Look at the chart," replied Mrs. Bernthal. "Whose name is down for this weekend?"

"Rachel had her last weekend," called out Matt Blakey. "So it's Robert's turn."

"Hey, Robert," said Paul. "You're lucky. You get Trudy for four days!"

Robert was pleased. He took Trudy's little cage and placed it next to his book bag on the table. Paul bent over and stroked Trudy through the bars of the cage. "Poor Trudy," he said. "Nick nearly drowned her when I had her at my house."

"How did he do that?" asked Robert.

"He tried to feed her from his bottle and she had milk all over her. Yuck! What a mess. But I cleaned her up and put her cage on a high shelf where Nick couldn't reach her."

What if something terrible happened while he had Trudy? Robert suddenly thought. Would he know what to do? Most of the class was on its way out the door, but Robert turned toward the classroom library. He passed Lester, who bellowed, "Happy Thanksgiving, Turkey!"

"Um . . . Happy Thanksgiving," answered Robert.

Lester hadn't bothered him since the underwear incident. Once in a while he called Robert a name. But there were no more fights.

Robert kept walking back to the library. He took *How to Raise a Happy Hamster* off the shelf. When he opened it, he saw that the first picture had a violet slash through it. The Scribbler had struck again!

He looked at the bulletin board where paper keys, like crisp fall leaves, were pinned with silver tacks. How would he ever win the treasure chest if he couldn't even take care of the class's books? He was the library monitor, and his job was to protect them. He had to get to the bottom of this. Mrs. Bernthal was counting on him.

Was Lester coming from the library just before he saw Robert? He was always causing trouble—maybe he was ruining the books, just to be mean.

Robert went over to Mrs. Bernthal's desk and looked up *How to Raise a Happy Hamster*

on the library list. The last time it was borrowed was two weeks before, and the borrower's
name was Paul Felcher.

The Other Side of Town

Once Robert got home, he opened Trudy's cage and put her on the coffee table. The first thing Trudy did was poop, right next to the glass polar bear. It was a good thing Robert's father wasn't home. Mr. Dorfman was a neat freak—Robert's mother said he couldn't help it. If someone moved the glass polar bear, even an inch, he moved it back again.

Robert cleaned up the mess and let Trudy loose on the living room floor. She scampered across the thick carpet toward the TV set. Robert grabbed her just as Charlie came in.

"Yo. What's this?" asked Charlie. "A mouse?"

"It's not a mouse," said Robert. "It's a hamster."

Charlie snickered and ran up the stairs to his room. "Mouse, hamster, it's the same thing."

Robert dropped Trudy into his shirt pocket with a few cookie crumbs. He heard Trudy munching on them. Then she tried climbing out, so Robert put her back in her cage and snapped the little door shut.

He had a box of hamster food that Mrs. Bernthal had sent home with him, but what else could he feed her? He liked giving Trudy things to munch on. He took out *How to Raise a Happy Hamster* from his book bag.

Chapter 3 was about food. The first word was long and hard: V-E-G-E-T-A-B-L-E-S. Robert sounded it out. "Veg-e-tables." Vegetables!

"Vegetables and grains are the basic foods for a heal-health-healthy hamster. A carrot stick or a let-lettuce leaf will provide . . ." Robert got stuck on another long word. N-O-U-R-I-S-H-M-E-N-T. It was harder than vegetables. He skipped over it and kept going.

"For special treats give your hamster small seeds or nuts. These foods will keep the hamster's teeth in good con-di-condition." The book did not mention cookie crumbs. Did hamsters

70

have to worry about the five food groups, too?

Robert heard a car in the driveway. He ran upstairs and put Trudy's cage on the desk in his room. He bounced down the stairs just as his father came in the door.

"Hello, Tiger," said his father.

"Hi, Dad."

"Gee, it's good to be home. I'm looking forward to four days off."

Robert's father went into the bedroom to change and when he came out, he had on jeans, a sweater, and sneakers. He settled into the recliner with his feet up, opened the newspaper, and fell asleep. Robert curled up on the sofa opposite his father and started reading about hamster babies in Chapter 5.

The phone rang, but Mr. Dorfman didn't move. Robert answered it, the way his mom had asked him to. "Dorfman residence, Robert speaking."

"Hello, Robert," said a woman's voice. "This is Mrs. Rodgers . . . Susanne Lee's mother? Is your mother home?"

"No," said Robert, "but my father is here."

"Oh," said Mrs. Rodgers. "May I speak to him, please?"

"Sure."

He put the phone down and went over to his father in the recliner. He shook his arm. "Dad?"

"Huh? What's up?"

"Dad, someone wants to speak to you," said Robert.

"Who?" The newspaper fell off Mr. Dorfman's lap onto the floor as he stood up.

"It's Susanne Lee Rodgers's mother," said Robert.

In a sleepy haze, Robert's father walked over to the phone. "Hello, Mrs. Rodgers?" he said. "Um, you probably want my wife. She—Oh? . . . At the school? . . . Oh, of course. Just wait right there. . . . Heh heh. That's true. What else can you do? I'm sorry. . . . I'll be right over." He hung up the phone.

"What's up, Dad?"

"Mrs. Rodgers is stuck over at the school. Her car won't start and she's supposed to deliver the Thanksgiving food basket."

"Can I come?"

"Sure, Tiger. Come on."

Mrs. Rodgers seemed very glad to see Robert and his father drive up. Hers was the only car in the school parking lot.

"Thanks so much," she cried, running over. "I don't know what I would have done if you weren't home. It's a holiday and everyone has left school. I found a phone across the street, but my husband had already left his office, and none of the other PTA parents are home."

"Glad to help," said Robert's father.

Mrs. Rodgers opened her car door and lifted out the Thanksgiving basket. "Almost everyone at the River Edge garage went home early for the holiday," she continued. "They don't have anyone to send over and can't even pick up my car until Friday. Can you imagine?"

"Don't worry," replied Robert's father. "We'll get you home." He took the basket and put it in the backseat of his car. Robert scooted in and sat next to it.

Turning to Robert, Mrs. Rodgers said, "Susanne Lee has told me so much about you. I'm glad we had a chance to meet."

What could Susanne Lee Rodgers possibly have to say about him? Robert wondered. That he was not such a great reader? That he put the wrong kind of food into the Thanksgiving basket? That he carried the tuba on Assembly mornings? Robert just smiled politely.

Mrs. Rodgers took a piece of paper from her purse and said to Robert's dad, "Fourteen Baxter Road. It's way on the other side of town, I'm afraid."

"That's O.K. We'll find it."

As they rode along, Robert noticed the houses were getting more run-down. They didn't have neatly trimmed hedges, and the leaves in the yards hadn't been raked or blown. In some of the backyards they passed, he could see old machinery and rusty cars.

"Make a right at the next corner," said Mrs. Rodgers.

A row of old gray houses with most of their paint peeled off lined the street.

"That's it right there," she said, pointing to a house with a sagging porch. In the yard, clothes flapped on a clothesline.

Robert stayed in the car and watched as the two grownups walked up the path to the front door with the food basket.

They rang the bell and a woman came to the door. Mrs. Rodgers said something, and the woman put a hand to her face. At once, children appeared, surrounding her. There were

five of them, but one—the biggest one—stood out. Robert thought his face seemed familiar, and then he realized it was Lester Willis.

Robert slunk down in his seat so Lester wouldn't see him. When his dad opened the car door for Mrs. Rodgers, Robert slipped farther down.

"Lose something, Tiger?" asked his dad. "There's a flashlight in the glove compartment."

"No, Dad, it's O.K."

At last they drove off. Robert waited a good long time before he sat up again.

Charlie to the Rescue

"Come on, Tiger!" Mr. Dorfman called, honking the horn. "We can't start Thanksgiving without you."

"Wait! I need my book!" Robert cried, running back into the house.

"O.K., but hurry," said his mother, holding the front door open.

Robert ran up to his room. Aunt Julie and Uncle Dan had no children. All they had was a cat named Phineas who was old and fat and no fun to play with. Whenever they visited, the grownups always talked for hours. Robert needed something to do so he wouldn't be bored.

He picked up *How to Raise a Happy Hamster* and saw Trudy staring up at him from her cage.

"So long, Trudy. We won't be gone long," he said. It was a lie and he knew it. He squeezed a few sunflower seeds through the bars of her cage. It was Thanksgiving, and the whole family would be together, but Trudy would be all alone for the entire day.

Robert opened the cage and lifted Trudy out. He meant just to say good-bye, but on an impulse he put her in his shirt pocket. He looked in his closet, his desk drawers, and his dresser drawers for something to put her in, and then he found the tissue box. He quickly pulled out most of the tissues and gently transferred Trudy to the box. It was the deep square kind, so she wouldn't be able to climb out too easily. Robert threw a few sunflower seeds into the box, put it in his book bag, and zipped the bag up only partway so Trudy could get some air.

"Come on, Robert. Your father's eager to get on the road," said his mother when he came downstairs.

"A whole book bag for one book?" Charlie was leaning against the car, arms folded. "You're one weird kid, you know that?"

Robert shrugged and went past him into the car.

In the backseat, Charlie stared out the window. He had his earphones on and drummed his fingers to music Robert could not hear. Robert reached down in his book bag and felt inside the tissue box. He patted Trudy's warm little bulge.

Robert's mother twisted around as far as the seat belt would let her. "I'm glad you're taking such an interest in reading, Robert," she said. Robert smiled and sat back in the seat. His mother's perfume drifted toward him and made him sleepy.

He thought about yesterday and Lester Willis. Mrs. Bernthal said that the food basket was going to a poor family, but it never occurred to him it might be someone he knew. Was Lester really poor? Robert had always imagined a homeless person when he thought of someone who was poor. But Lester's family wasn't homeless.

The car ride to Connecticut was long, and Robert slept through most of it. At last they pulled into Aunt Julie's driveway.

She met them at the door and hugged and kissed everybody. Then Uncle Dan led them down the hall to the bedroom. "Throw your coats on the bed," he said. Robert put his jacket on the bed and his book bag on top of all the coats. He opened the zipper a tiny bit to be sure Trudy could breathe.

All day long, Robert sneaked away to visit Trudy. He brought her a raw string bean that he stole from a pile on the kitchen table. He popped a couple of grapes off the fruit arrangement on the coffee table and brought them to Trudy when no one was looking.

After dinner, the grownups had coffee and talked. After they cleared the table, the men excused themselves and went to the living room to watch a football game while Robert's mom and Aunt Julie continued talking.

Robert went to the bedroom to give Trudy some piecrust crumbs. When he reached deep into his book bag, he didn't feel anything warm and furry. Trudy was gone!

He felt around again and looked inside. A whole corner of the tissue box had been chewed up into lots of shredded paper. Luckily, the hamster book underneath was not damaged.

Robert looked around. Trudy was loose somewhere in the house, but how would he find her? Aunt Julie would probably faint if she found out.

Robert remembered reading that hamsters like warm hiding places. Maybe Trudy was behind the stove—it would be warm there.

He went out to the kitchen and looked under the stove. There was nothing there. Then he thought he heard a scratching noise. He listened. It seemed to be coming from behind the refrigerator. Robert put his face right up to the space between the refrigerator and the wall and tried to look back there.

"What are you doing?" Charlie asked. Robert jumped.

"Nothing," he said.

"Oh? You always look behind people's refrigerators?"

Robert shrugged.

"Rob, you're being weird again. Why don't you just tell me what you're doing?"

"No! Go away." Robert hadn't trusted Charlie since the toilet incident.

"Did you lose something back there?"

"Maybe. Maybe not."

Charlie took the broom from the corner of the kitchen.

Robert panicked. "What are you going to do?"

"I want to see what's back there," said Charlie.

"No, don't. I'll tell you," Robert said, giving in. He didn't want Charlie to hurt Trudy. "It's Trudy, the hamster. I brought her with me and she got loose."

"The mouse? Boy, Rob, you sure are full of surprises! You have to get her out before Aunt Julie finds out," said Charlie.

"I know. Maybe she'll come out if I put these down." He dropped the pumpkin-pie crumbs on the floor near the refrigerator and waited quietly.

For a split second, Robert saw Trudy's little head peek out. "She's there! I saw her!" Robert tried not to speak above a whisper. He didn't want his parents or Aunt Julie and Uncle Dan to hear.

Then Phineas came trotting in, looking for some turkey leftovers, and Robert had an awful thought. What if Phineas got to Trudy before he did? What would he tell his class? "I'm sorry, but Trudy was somebody's Thanksgiving dinner"?

82

"She'll never come out with Phineas here," said Charlie.

"Let's lock Phineas in the bedroom," said Robert.

"No," said Charlie. "He might make a racket and everyone will come running."

A roll of aluminum foil was on the counter. Charlie took a piece off the roll and crumpled it into a ball. He knelt down and batted it in front of Phineas, who immediately leaped at the moving silver ball.

"You keep playing with Phineas while I move the fridge," said Charlie, standing up and handing Robert the foil.

"You can't move the refrigerator!" Robert cried.

"I'm just going to wiggle it out a little."

Charlie heaved and the refrigerator moved. The small space was now almost big enough for Robert to fit into.

"Keep Phineas busy," Charlie said, picking up the broom.

"What are you going to do?" Robert cried.

"Don't worry. I won't hurt her. I'll just ease her out with the broom. When she comes out, yell, and I'll grab her. You keep an eye on Phineas."

Robert nodded and kept rolling the silver ball in front of the cat, who did not take his eyes off it.

Charlie bent down and poked the broom under the refrigerator. He moved it slowly from one end of the refrigerator to the other. Suddenly a little fur ball waddled out.

"There she goes!" said Robert. "Get her!"

Charlie grabbed Trudy just as Phineas saw her. He handed her to Robert, who dropped Trudy safely into his shirt pocket.

Charlie got the refrigerator back in place just as Aunt Julie walked in.

"Hi, boys. Want some apple cider?" she asked, opening the refrigerator.

"No, thanks," they said at the same time.

As Aunt Julie turned around with the cider jug in her hand, Trudy popped her head out of Robert's pocket. Aunt Julie's mouth dropped open.

"Robert!" she cried. "What's in your pocket?"

Robert's knees felt weak. "A hamster," he said.

"Well, for goodness sake. Dan! Dan, come here," Aunt Julie called.

Uncle Dan hurried into the kitchen.

"Look at what Robert has in his pocket!"

Uncle Dan stared at Robert's pocket. "What is it? A rat?"

"No, dear, it's a hamster," said Aunt Julie. "Isn't it adorable?"

Robert couldn't believe his ears.

"What's going on?" asked Robert's father, coming in.

"It's Robert's hamster," explained Aunt Julie.

"Oh!" said Mrs. Dorfman, joining them. "Robert, why did you bring that creature with you?"

"Please don't be mad at him," said Aunt Julie. "Robert is a thoughtful boy to take his hamster with him. It isn't bothering anyone."

Robert's mother tried to say something, but Aunt Julie wouldn't let her. "Remember, Clare, the hamster we had once?" she said. "Maybe you were too young to remember. His name was Nutmeg, and I took him everywhere with me. They sent me home from school one day when Nutmeg fell out of my pocket during a spelling bee and frightened Miss Brundage out of her skin."

Robert's mother smiled.

"I don't think we have a picture of Nutmeg," Aunt Julie told Robert, "but tell your mother to show you the picture of us with the frogs sometime."

Robert looked over at his mother. Now she was laughing. "Yes," said Mrs. Dorfman. "I remember those pictures. They're in a photo album somewhere."

"Your mother was the best frog catcher in our town," Aunt Julie told Robert and Charlie. "She used to sell them to the other kids for a quarter each and then have races for a prize."

Robert couldn't imagine his mother and Aunt Julie as little girls. He wanted to see those pictures.

"Ah, so that's where she got her head for business," said Mr. Dorfman.

On the ride home, Robert looked over at Charlie, who had his earphones on again. He sure was strong and smart, and he helped rescue Trudy. Robert reached into the shoebox

Aunt Julie had given him to replace the tissue box and wrapped his hand around Trudy.

"Want to hold her?" he asked, offering the hamster to Charlie.

Charlie's eyes opened wide. "Sure," he said. He took Trudy and stroked her little head. "Thanks," he said, handing her back to Robert.

Robert carefully put Trudy in the shoebox, leaned back, and slept all the way home.

Something Fishy

On Monday morning, Robert returned Trudy's cage to the window sill and put *How to Raise a Happy Hamster* on Mrs. Bernthal's desk.

"Thank you, Robert. Did you read the book?" Mrs. Bernthal asked.

"Um . . . I don't know. I . . . I don't think so," said Robert.

"What do you mean?"

"Well, I read the chapter about food. Then I read another chapter about hamster babies. Then I went back to read about hamster houses. I read all the chapters, but I mixed them up."

"Well, reading a book from cover to cover doesn't mean you have to read it in order," said Mrs. Bernthal. "Some books are like that. You can read them any which way at all."

"Way to go," cried Paul from his seat.

"Um . . . Mrs. Bernthal . . ."

"Yes, Robert?"

"There's a purple scribble in this book. But I didn't do it."

"Oh no!" cried Mrs. Bernthal, flipping through it. "Another book has been ruined!" Her lips were in a tight line and her cheeks were red. "I must put a stop to this," she told the class. "You don't have to tattle. We will use the honor system. Whoever did this to our books can tell me privately. Nobody else has to know, and I will be very fair."

Mrs. Bernthal closed the book. "Until then," she said, "there will be no more recess. We will write in our journals instead. Perhaps that will give you time to reflect on your responsibilities."

Robert looked at Paul drawing an astronaut in his notebook. He had taken the hamster book out before Robert. How come he hadn't noticed the scribbles?

When Robert's class went to the art room that afternoon, Miss Valentine met them out in the hall. She held a tissue over her nose.

"Don't go in!" she called, and Robert and the other boys and girls behind him stopped short. There was a terrible smell coming from the room. Mike, the school janitor, came out holding a plastic trash bag out in front of him.

"Pee-yew!" said Paul.

"It's dead, whatever it is," said Matt Blakey.

"You mean . . . it's a dead animal?" said Robert.

"More like dead *fish*," said Miss Valentine. She looked straight at Robert and held up a can of Floral Bouquet Room Freshener to spray into the air. "Remember the great cleanup you did on Wednesday?" she asked, frowning.

Robert gulped. "Yes," he said.

"Well," said Miss Valentine, "you put the fish we used for the fish prints in the supply cabinet with the other supplies, Robert. They have been rotting for four days over the long weekend."

"Eee-ew! Rotten fish!" the class moaned. Everyone spun around and gagged at the idea. Vanessa pretended she was going to upchuck, and Susanne Lee made a terrible face.

Miss Valentine shot another stream of Floral Bouquet into the air. Some children ducked the

spray, while others screamed or held their noses.

"You will just have to go back to Mrs. Bernthal's room," said Miss Valentine. "We can't work in here until this room is fumigated."

"Fumigate Robert!" shouted Lester. "Pee-yew!"

"AAAARGH!" yelled Matt Blakey, pretending he was passing out from the smell.

When Robert walked near Janice Lambert on the way back to their classroom, she cried, "Oh no, it's Robert!" and ran by quickly, holding her nose.

For the rest of the day, everyone except Paul acted as if *he* smelled bad instead of the art room. Miss Valentine would probably fire him, Robert thought.

"Settle down, class," said Mrs. Bernthal. "While the art room is closed, let's use this time to go over our multiplication tables."

Math. It couldn't get any worse than this.

Getting Warmer

After the longest day Robert could remember, the bell rang and everyone scrambled for their coats. Robert put all the chairs up on the tables as usual.

Paul was waiting for him at the door.

"You better go ahead," Robert said. "I want to work on the books."

"O.K., Super Helper," Paul said with a smile. He gave a little wave as he left.

Robert moved toward the library shelves. Just running his hands across all those smooth covers made him feel better. He now had the authors arranged from A to Z. Mrs. Bernthal had helped him. There were different sections for science and nature, places, biographies, poetry, and fun and games. There was even a special section for easy readers.

As he turned the corner of the bookcase wall, he was startled to see Lester on the floor. Lester quickly stuffed something into his book bag. An open book lay on the floor next to it that was covered with green scribbles.

"What are you doing?" asked Robert.

"None of your business," answered Lester. He got up from the floor.

"It is my business," said Robert. "I'm the library monitor, and I saw you put something in your book bag." He was sure it was a marker.

"Yeah? So what?"

"So you're ruining our books!" He was so glad to know it wasn't Paul!

"How would you like a fat lip?"

"I'm sorry, but it's my job. I have to stop you from ruining any more books!"

"I didn't ruin any books!"

"Then show me your book bag," said Robert, feeling his knees shake.

"Get out of my way!" said Lester.

Robert didn't budge. After all, he had a job to do, and he was someone who cared. "You have to tell Mrs. Bernthal . . . ," he said, his voice coming out in a whisper.

Lester put his face up against Robert's. "OR WHAT?" he boomed.

Robert couldn't believe how wobbly his legs were now. This might be his last moment on earth. He thought of praying—*Now I lay me down to sleep* . . .

"Or I could tell . . ." Robert remembered Lester's pink underwear, but telling about that might make Lester even angrier. He thought about dropping off the food basket at Lester's house. But he couldn't tell everyone that. Maybe some kids would laugh, but being poor wasn't something to laugh at.

". . . and Mrs. Bernthal won't let you take any books home." It sounded so lame he almost laughed himself.

Lester backed off. Robert could breathe again.

Lester put his book bag down and unzipped it. Out spilled his notebook, a math workbook, some stubby pencils, a comic book, and an easy reader about Frog and Toad from the class library.

Robert picked up the book and looked through it. It had no scribbles. Then he looked down at the bag and asked, "Where are the markers?"

"What markers?" said Lester.

"The ones you're marking the books with," said Robert.

"I told you!" said Lester, getting angry again. "I didn't ruin the books!"

"Then what are you doing here?"

"I was just . . . borrowing a book, that's all."

"Why didn't you just sign it out with Mrs. Bernthal?"

"Yeah. Sure. So everyone can see I read baby books." Lester got sulky again.

"You really mean it? You didn't scribble in the books?"

Lester's frown deepened. "That's what I told you. I didn't do it."

Robert looked at *Frog and Toad Are Friends*. He remembered what a great day it was for him when he was first able to read one of the chapters by himself. He believed Lester was telling the truth.

"I can let you take out this book without signing Mrs. Bernthal's list."

Lester, still frowning, stared at Robert. "You can?"

"Sure. I'll put my name down for it." He handed the book back to Lester, who slipped it into his book bag.

"You will? And you won't tell anyone?"

Robert shrugged. "Why would I do that? All I want is to find the Scribbler."

"Yeah. Someone's really messing up the books."

Robert watched as Lester picked up his book bag and walked away. That left Paul as the prime suspect.

"I have some good news," said Robert's mother that night as she set out a plate of fruit for dessert.

The only really good news, Robert thought, would be that he wouldn't have to go back to school ever again. He wished he had never taken the job of library monitor. He liked working with the books, but now he had to be a tattle-tale. He pulled a grape off the bunch.

"Did you win the lottery?" asked Robert's father.

"No. It's better than that," said Robert's mother. "The Dorfmans are going on a family fun vacation!"

"We are?" said Charlie.

"When?" asked Robert's father.

"I realized we need a little family fun of our own, and I thought we could begin planning for next summer. You three are off, and Ginny said she'd cover for me at the office. What would you guys think of going to Disney World?"

"Yo, Mom!" said Charlie.

Robert stared at his family, who sat grinning all around him.

"Robert? Aren't you pleased?" asked his mother.

He managed a smile. "Sure, Mom, it's great. Really!" But even Disney World couldn't change the facts. Paul must be the Scribbler after all, and Robert had to figure out how to turn in his best friend.

Caught
in the Act

On Tuesday morning, Robert felt as if there was a rock in his stomach. When Mrs. Bernthal handed out the previous day's homework, GOOD WORK was stamped on top of Robert's paper, with a picture of a beaver in a hard hat. Robert couldn't help himself and shouted, "YES!" Mrs. Bernthal laughed in surprise. Two days in a row he had received an A on his homework! Then Robert looked over at Paul, and the awful feeling in his stomach came back.

"Take out your journals," said Mrs. Bernthal, sitting down at her desk. "I'd like you to write in them until you leave for music. You have about twenty minutes."

Robert wrote as neatly as he could: My best friend Paul is

The line stared back at him and made his stomach hurt even more. He finished the sentence: My best friend Paul is a good artist.

He couldn't write what he was really thinking—it was just too terrible. The twenty minutes were up, and Robert had not written another word.

Robert always sat with Paul in the lunchroom until it was time to help Mrs. Ruskin, but today he hesitated.

"You go ahead," he said to Paul. "I have to do something."

"O.K.," said Paul. "See you later."

Robert saw Lester sitting by himself. He went over to Lester's table and sat down across from him.

"You want to eat with me?" asked Lester, taking a bite of his sandwich.

Robert looked over at Paul, who was laughing with Brian and Jesse and Matt. He wished he could be there with them, laughing over their latest jokes. Then he looked at Lester—he didn't seem so tough now. "Sure," he said, taking out his sandwich. "I'm sorry I thought you were the Scribbler."

Lester stopped chewing. "Well, just remember, you made a promise about—you know—the books." He glanced around to make sure no one else could hear.

"Don't worry, I'll keep my promise," Robert replied.

"What do you have?" asked Lester, leaning his big head over Robert's sandwich.

"Turkey."

Lester looked pleased. "Me, too." He rolled up his empty lunch bag and threw it on the floor. Robert stared at it. He wanted to pick up the paper bag, but he sat still.

"I . . . I have an idea," he said.

"Yeah? Like what?" asked Lester, studying Robert suspiciously.

"I can save the books I read for you. Then I can help you if you have trouble with any of the words."

"You mean it?" Lester's jaw continued to work as he spoke. He pulled out a small plastic bag and offered a chocolate-covered jelly cookie to Robert.

Robert took one and bit into it. "Sure. There's a book you'll like that's not too hard. It's about moths."

"Hey, that's cool!" said Lester. He rolled up the plastic bag, but Robert grabbed it before he threw it on the floor.

"The trash barrel isn't very far," Robert explained.

Lester punched Robert on the arm in a friendly way. Robert smiled and got up to go to Mrs. Ruskin's room, rubbing his arm.

"Yo. Rob," said Lester.

"What?"

"My . . . um . . . underwear?"

"Yeah?"

"My sister did the laundry one day and her red shirt turned everything pink."

Robert shrugged. "Women," he said.

Lester just grinned.

"Want to come to my house?" asked Paul on the way home from school.

"I don't know," answered Robert. "I have a lot of stuff to do."

"What kind of stuff?"

"You know. Homework, and . . ."

"We have the same homework," Paul replied. "We can do it together."

Robert shifted his book bag on his back. "O.K. For a little while. I have to tell you something."

"What?" said Paul.

"I thought Lester Willis was the Scribbler."

"Yeah. So?"

"Well, I'm pretty sure now he's not."

"How come?"

"I just don't think Lester would do it. I know he's tough, and sometimes he's a bully, but he wouldn't ruin our books."

"Well, someone must have a real problem, doing that to our books."

"That's for sure," Robert said, kicking a stone on the sidewalk.

Paul's mother had Oreos and milk for them. "Robert," she said, "it's nice to see you so clean for a change." They both laughed. After a snack and a phone call home, Robert followed Paul upstairs to his room. "Be right back," said Paul, dropping his book bag on the floor. "I need a bathroom break."

While he was gone, Robert looked at some new drawings on the wall over Paul's bed that were labeled "Asteroid Man." An astronaut in a blue streamlined spacesuit with a jagged gold stripe across his chest flew in and out among the planets. Robert thought it was amazing how Paul could make Asteroid Man look so real.

Robert sighed. If he could only find some reason to think he was wrong about Paul. But the more he looked at all those bright colors in the drawings, the more he was convinced that Paul had to be the Scribbler.

"Hi," said a voice. It was Nick, standing in the bedroom doorway.

"Hi, Nick. You looking for Paul?"

Nick smiled and toddled over to Paul's desk. He grabbed something and ran off with it.

A light went on in Robert's head. "Nick? What did you take?" he cried, running out the door after him. Nick was already in his own room grabbing a picture book. He had a red marker in his hand.

"Hey, no!" said Robert, lunging for the marker before Nick did any damage. Nick, surprised, almost began to cry, but Robert was faster. "Let's read a story," he said, taking the book from Nick. He sat down on the circus carpet and Nick fell into a heap beside him, sucking his thumb.

Paul came in as they were reading *Curious George*. "I didn't know you liked that book," he said, grinning.

"Paul! Wait till you hear! I found the Scribbler!" He held up the red marker and pointed it at Nick, who just laughed.

Treasure Chest Day

Robert couldn't get his hair to stay down. He brushed and brushed, but one clump kept sticking up. He sprayed some of Charlie's mousse on his hair, and a big glob that looked like whipped cream sat on his head. He wiped it off with a towel and rubbed in what was left. Then he brushed his hair again, and the clump stayed down. It was important to look nice because today was Treasure Chest Day.

Yesterday, before he left the classroom, Robert counted the paper keys on the bulletin board with his name on them. There were twenty-four. Susanne Lee Rodgers had twenty-five. After Mrs. Bernthal handed out the last paper keys for the week, they would know who won the gold chest.

When Robert and Paul got to school, the classroom was buzzing with excitement. Susanne Lee had curled her hair so it bounced even more than usual. She wore a watch. Susanne Lee even *looked* smart.

Mrs. Bernthal rapped on her desk. "I want you to know how proud of you I am," she said. "You all tried hard for the treasure chest. In trying, you learned more about yourselves, and you found out that you could do much more than you thought you could."

Mrs. Bernthal was right about that. Robert never thought he could read a book all by himself. Or get GOOD WORK stamped on his homework for a whole week!

Mrs. Bernthal began pulling down keys from the bulletin board to count them and called out names and accomplishments. Susanne Lee's name was called several times. Robert's hopes rose and fell several times.

"Robert Dorfman," called Mrs. Bernthal. Robert sat up straight. "I forgot to mention that you were Miss Valentine's helper this week. And," she added, "I'm giving you one for showing remarkable improvement in your work habits." Robert blinked and smiled. "You have been handing in much neater homework papers lately." Mrs. Bernthal added two more paper keys with Robert's name on them to the pile.

"Lester, you get one, too."

"Me?" said Lester.

"Yes, you," said Mrs. Bernthal. "I'm very proud of you for the improvement you have shown in your reading."

"Yo! I got a key!" Lester shouted.

"According to my tally," said Mrs. Bernthal after counting up the piles of keys, "the winner of the treasure chest is . . ." She looked at her chart and counted. Robert held his breath. "Susanne Lee Rodgers, with twenty-eight keys."

Susanne Lee bounced up to the front of the room and accepted the little gold box from Mrs. Bernthal. She held it up for everyone to see, and the class applauded.

Robert expected to feel a sharp stab of jealousy when he saw Susanne Lee with the treasure chest, but it didn't happen. She's so used to winning, Robert thought. What must it feel like, to win all the time?

"Your name will be engraved on it," Mrs. Bernthal told Susanne Lee. "I'll take it to the shop at lunchtime and see that it's done. You can pick it up at the end of the day and take it home with you."

"Thank you, Mrs. Bernthal," said Susanne Lee.

"I have one more announcement, class," said Mrs. Bernthal once Susanne Lee was back in her seat. "Robert, come up here." Robert knew she was calling him, but he couldn't move. "Come, Robert. I know you already received your paper keys each week for being library monitor, but I want you to know that we appreciate you for turning our library into a very special place. Not only did you solve the problem of our Scribbler"—she winked at Paul—"but the children use the books more, and the shelves are always neat and tidy. You have done an excellent job, and I believe you have earned this." She held out a rolled-up paper.

Robert's cheeks felt warm. He wondered if they were bright red. "Should . . . should I open it?" he asked.

"Yes, please do," Mrs. Bernthal answered.

Robert unrolled the paper, which read:

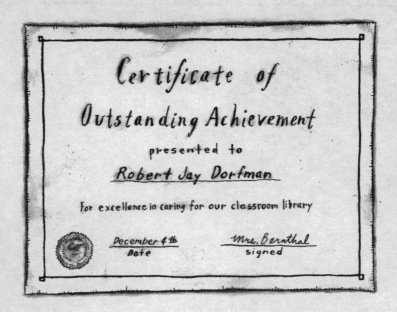

Certificate of
Outstanding Achievement
presented to
Robert Jay Dorfman

For excellence in caring for our classroom library

December 4th
Date

Mrs. Bernthal
signed

The certificate reminded Robert of what his father had told him, about how important it was to be a person who cares.

Paul, back at table four, shouted, "YES!" and the whole class whistled and applauded. Lester called out, "Way to go, Rob!"

Robert couldn't believe it. Everyone was looking at him and smiling, even Susanne Lee. For the first time, he understood how she felt. Maybe he didn't get the treasure chest, but he knew what it was like to be a winner.

At three o'clock, Robert carefully rolled up his certificate and put it in his book bag. He stopped at the library to place the loose books back on the shelves. Lester was looking at the pictures in a book about sharks.

"Hi, Lester."

"Yo," answered Lester.

"That one looks good. I was thinking of reading that myself. I can sign it out for you."

"Yeah. Thanks." Lester stuffed the book in his book bag and left.

Walking home, Robert couldn't find a good way to tell Paul what he had to. Finally, he just blurted it out, to get it over with. "I thought you were the Scribbler."

Paul stopped short. "How come?"

Robert stopped, too. "Well, you had all those markers, and some of the scribbles were the same colors as your markers. And the scribbles showed up in books that you'd borrowed. Anyway, I'm sorry."

Paul shook his head. "You would make a good detective!" He paused, then said, "I have something to tell you, too."

"What?" asked Robert.

"I thought your parents were getting a divorce."

"What gave you THAT idea?" cried Robert.

"Well . . . your mother was never home, and then you weren't going to have a Thanksgiving."

"Wait a minute!" Robert spun around and walked backward to face Paul. "My mother works. She gets pretty busy sometimes, and she had to take a trip, but we had a terrific Thanksgiving, with turkey and pie and everything. It was just at my aunt Julie's house." Robert kicked at a stone, and it went flying. "Why didn't you tell me what you thought?" he asked.

"I don't know," said Paul. "Why didn't you tell me you thought I was the Scribbler?"

"I don't know."

Robert stared at Paul.

Paul stared at Robert.

They started to laugh. "My mom always tells me I jump to conclusions," said Paul.

"What does that mean?" asked Robert.

"I think it means what we did," Paul replied. "Thinking something is true without checking it out."

"Yeah. That's what we did, all right," said Robert. He laughed some more.

"I guess we should ask next time, right?" said Paul.

"Right!" said Robert.

When Robert heard his father's key turn in the front door, he ran for his certificate. He stood in the doorway holding it open in front of him.

"Hi, Tiger," said his father.

"Hi," said Robert.

"What's this?" asked Mr. Dorfman, putting his briefcase down and coming closer to read it. "Robert! This is excellent!" said his father. "What did you do to earn it?"

"I took care of the books in our class library," said Robert. They sat down and Robert told him all about the paper keys and the treasure chest, the Scribbler, Lester, and Mrs. Bernthal surprising him with the special certificate.

Robert's father put his arm around his shoulders and gave him a quick squeeze. "I'm sure you can do anything, Tiger," he said. "Once you had a problem with your reading, and now look at you! You are in charge of an entire library!"

Mr. Dorfman got up and opened the desk drawer. He took out a frame, opened the back, and slid out a faded print. In its place he slipped Robert's certificate and replaced the glass. "There! It fits!" he said. "What do you think?" He held it up. Robert thought it looked beautiful. He watched as his father got the hammer and a nail and hung it on the living room wall.

That night at dinner Robert had to explain all over again about the certificate and the treasure chest and everything else for his mother and Charlie. He didn't mind one bit.